THROUGH THE MAGIC MIRROR
Anthony Browne

PUFFIN BOOKS

Toby sat in the big chair. He was fed up. Fed up with
books, fed up with toys, fed up with everything.

He went into the living room. Nothing was happening there.

Going back upstairs, he
saw himself in a mirror.

Something looked very strange
What was wrong?

He put out his hand to touch the mirror – and walked right through it!

He was out in the street. It seemed like the same old street, but was it?

An invisible man passed by.

On the corner was an easel. On the easel was
a painting of a painting of a painting.

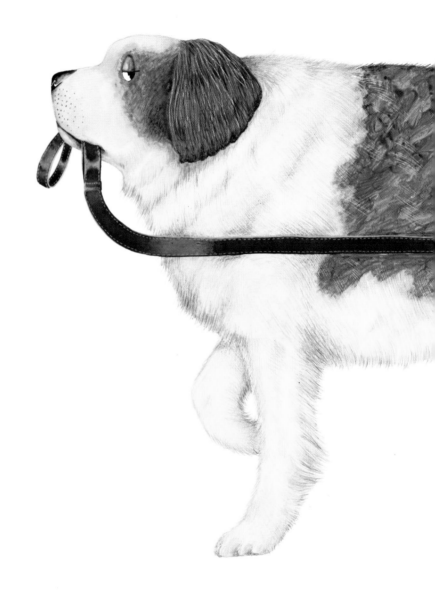

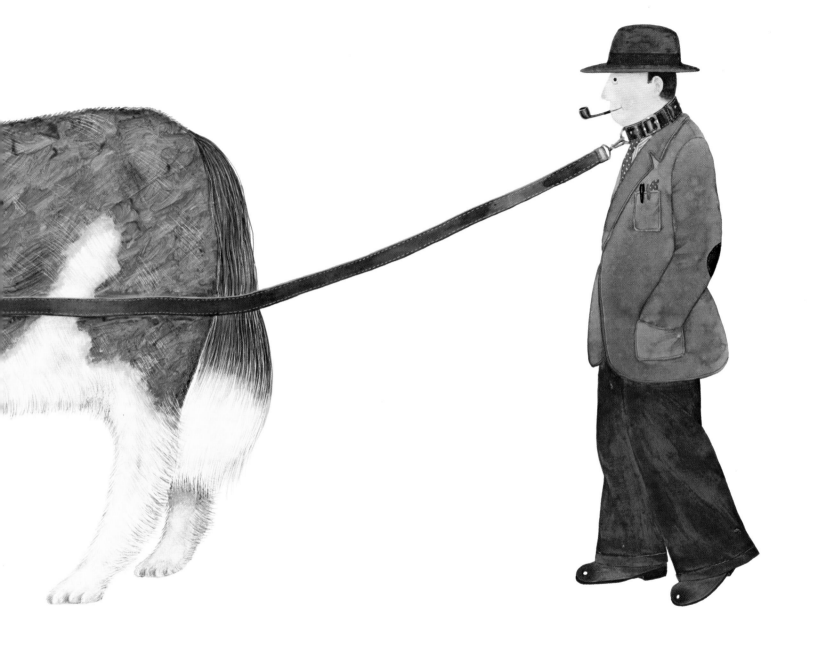

Just then a dog came along, taking a man for a walk.

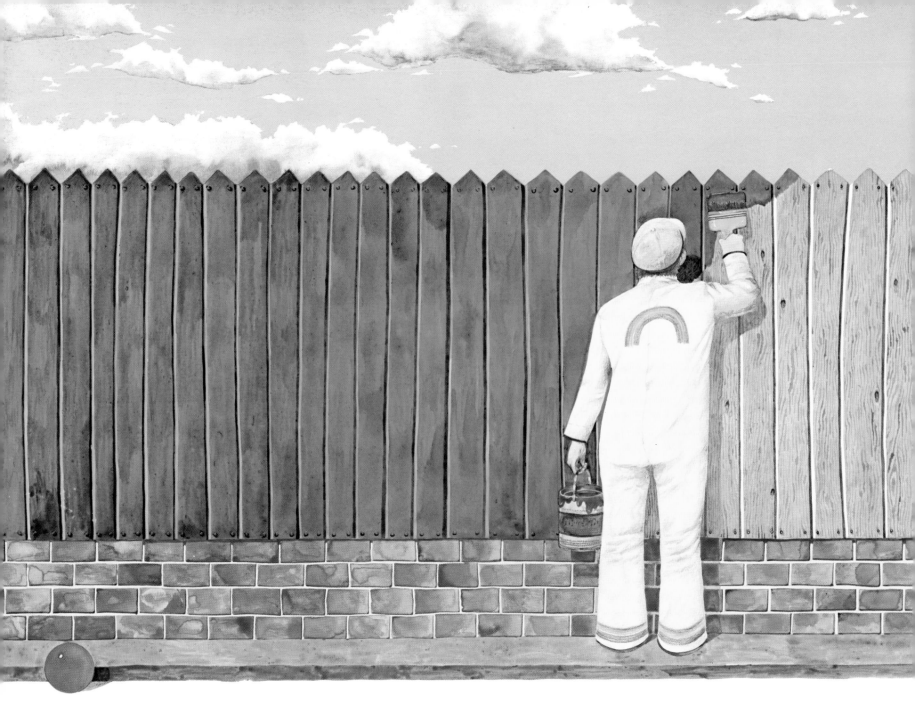

Toby walked on. Two men were painting a fence.

Toby took another look. He could hardly believe what he saw.

Suddenly the sky became dark as a flock of choirboys flew overhead.

A terrified cat darted past, chased by a gang of hungry mice.

At the bus stop Toby saw a queue of funny people.

They seemed a bit mixed up.

And the traffic seemed somehow different.

Across the road Toby saw a poster for the zoo.

But what was happening?

Toby ran as fast as he could.

Where was that mirror?

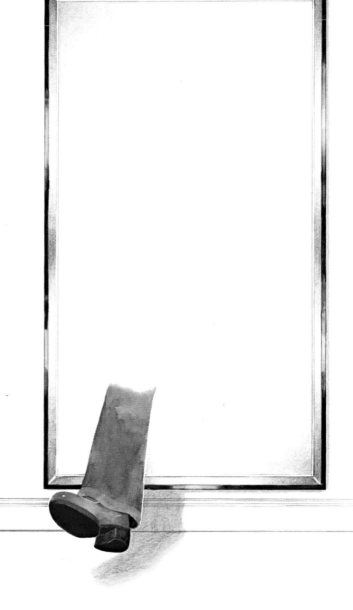

Of course, there it was, right behind him.

Toby stepped through, back into his own house.

He turned around and looked at himself in the mirror.
When he saw his face, he smiled.

Then he ran down to tea.